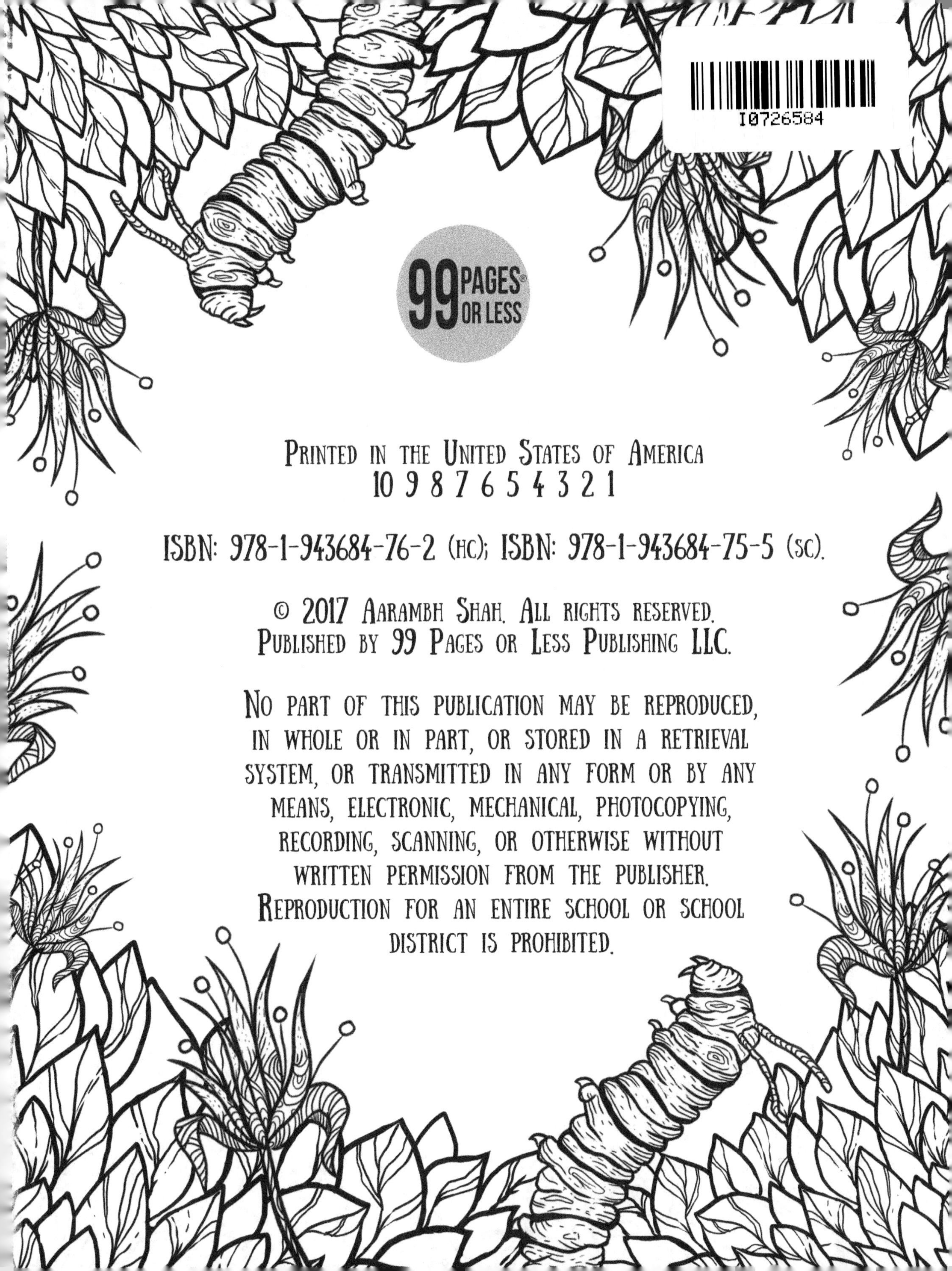

PRINTED IN THE UNITED STATES OF AMERICA
10 9 8 7 6 5 4 3 2 1

ISBN: 978-1-943684-76-2 (HC); ISBN: 978-1-943684-75-5 (SC).

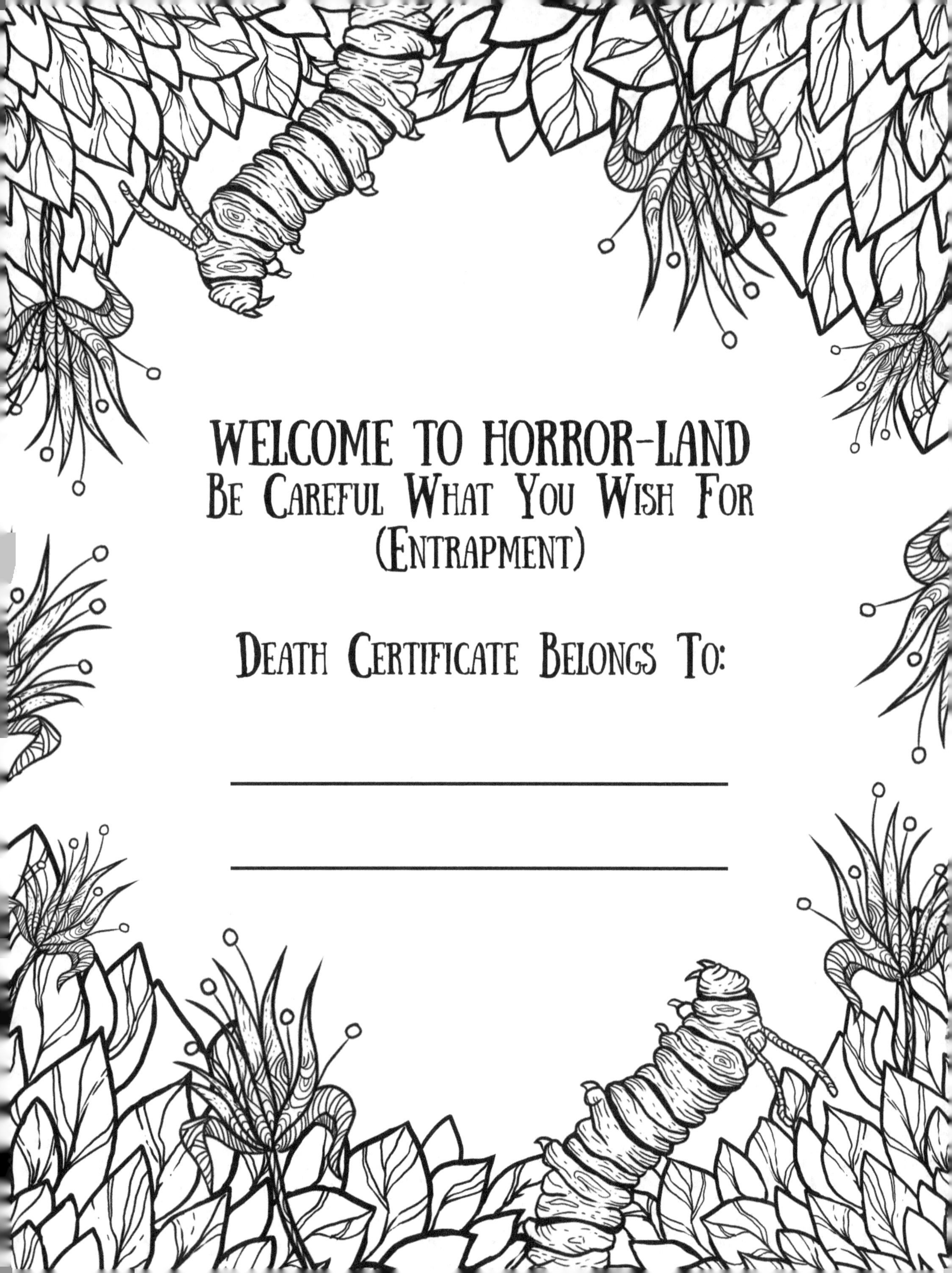

WELCOME TO HORROR-LAND
Be Careful What You Wish For
(Entrapment)

Death Certificate Belongs To:

____

____

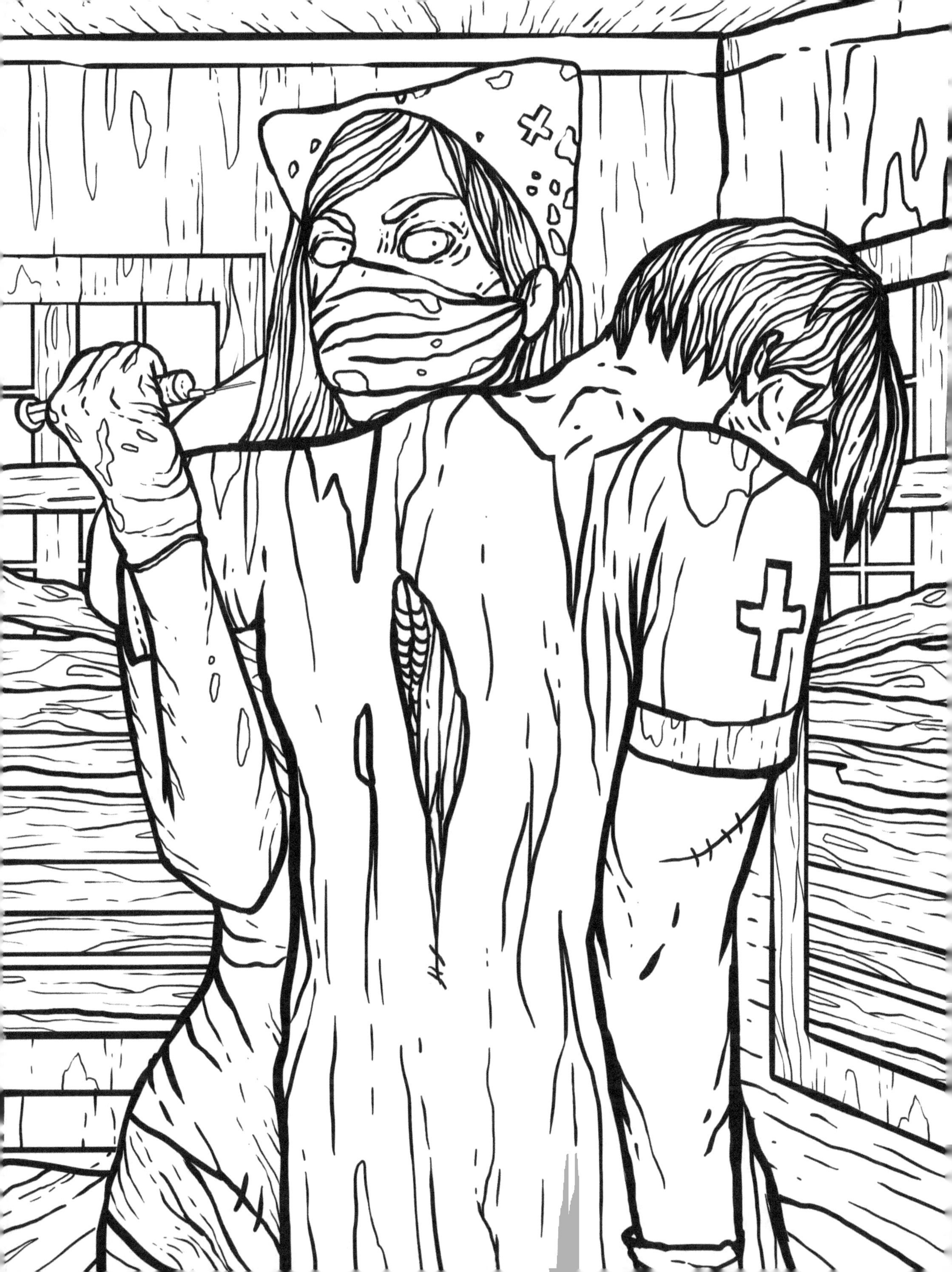

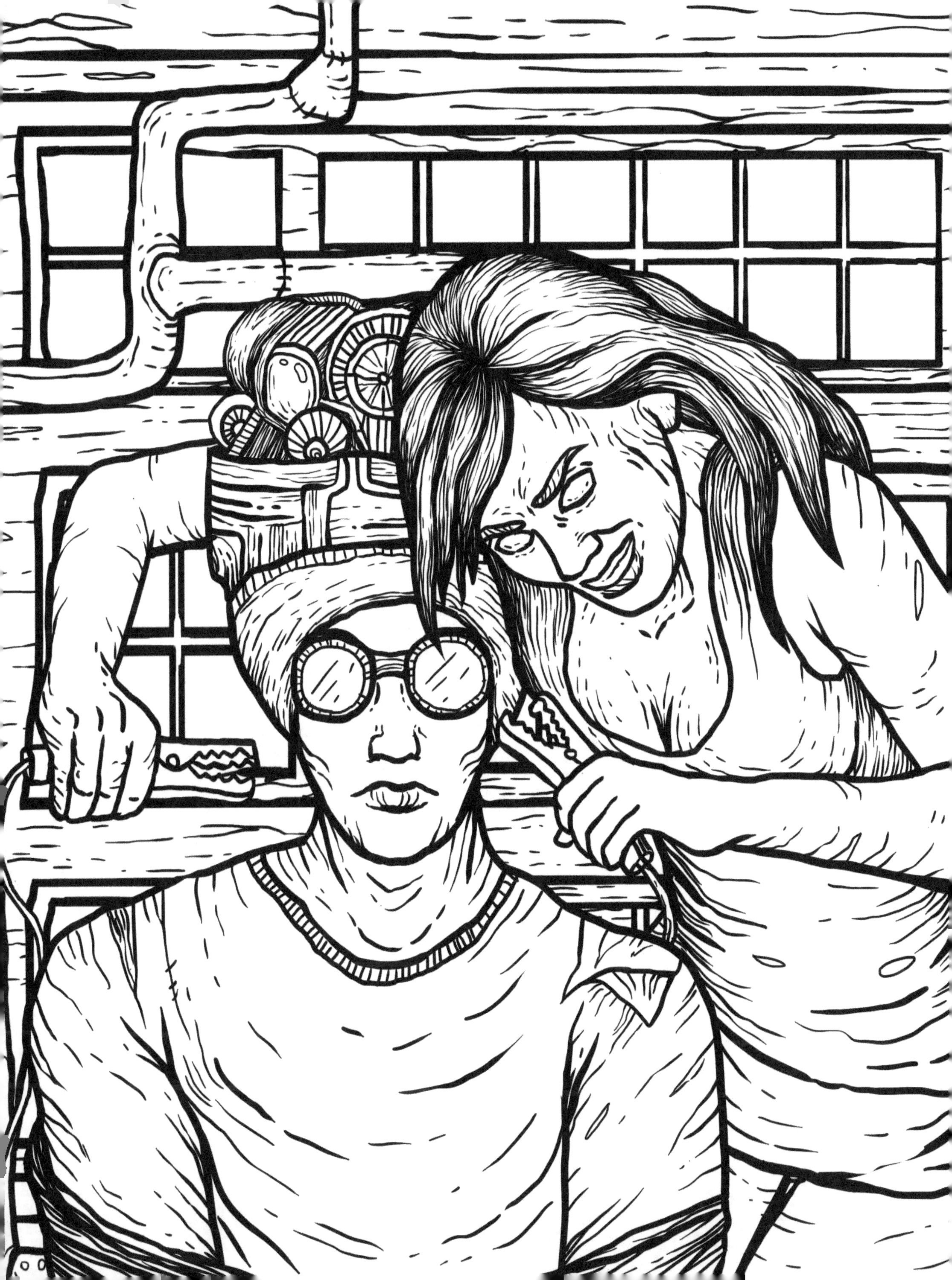

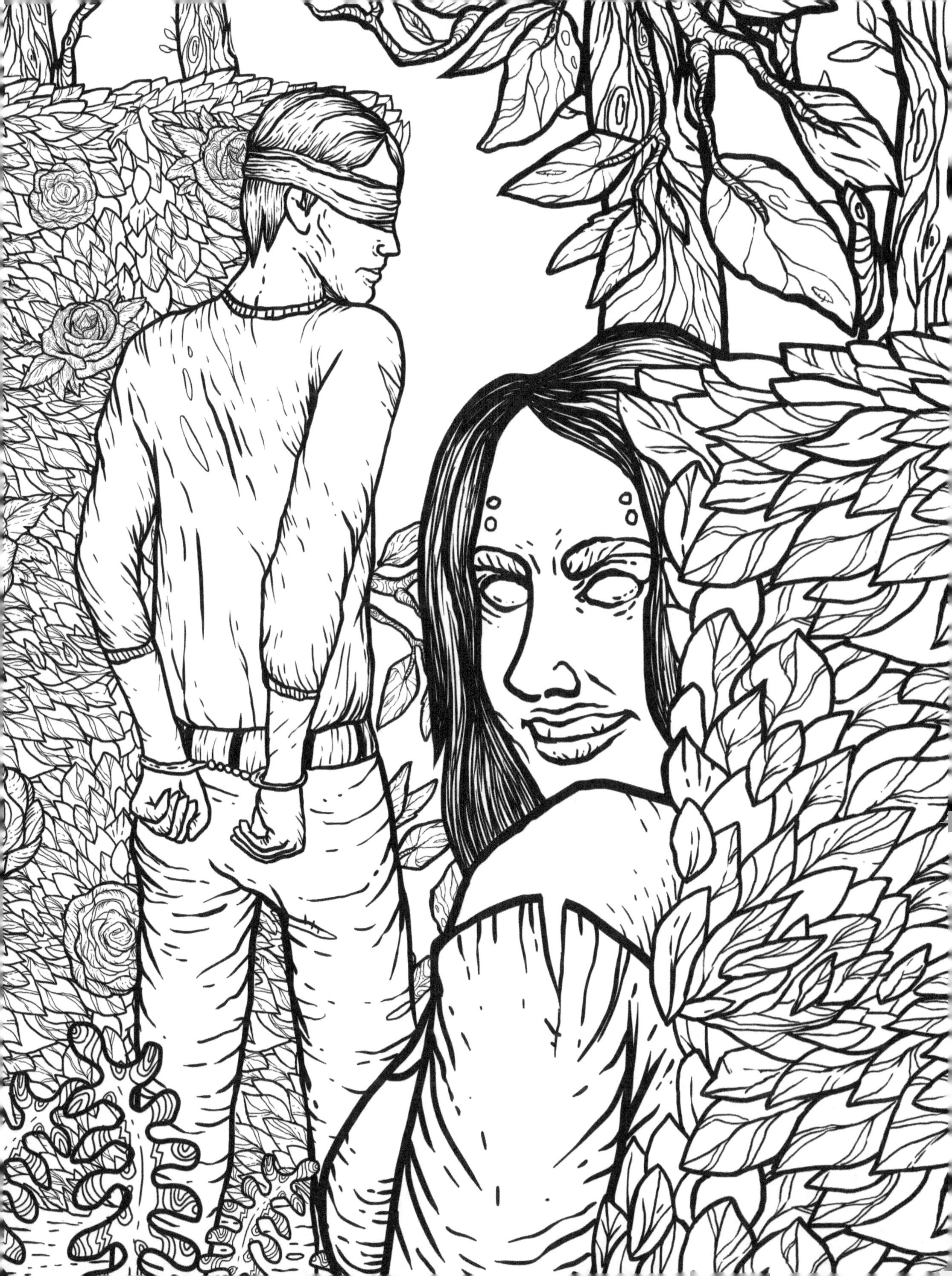

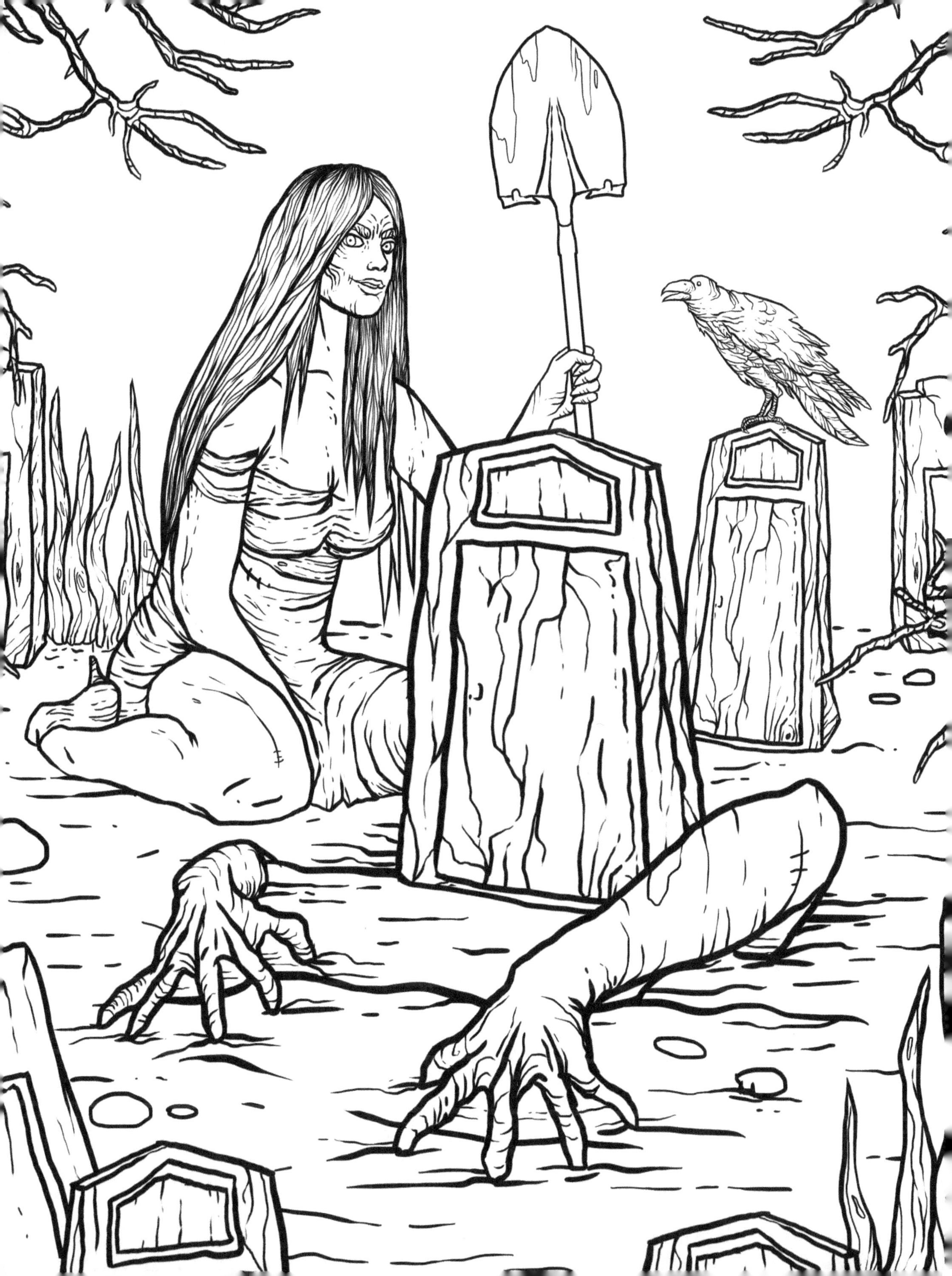

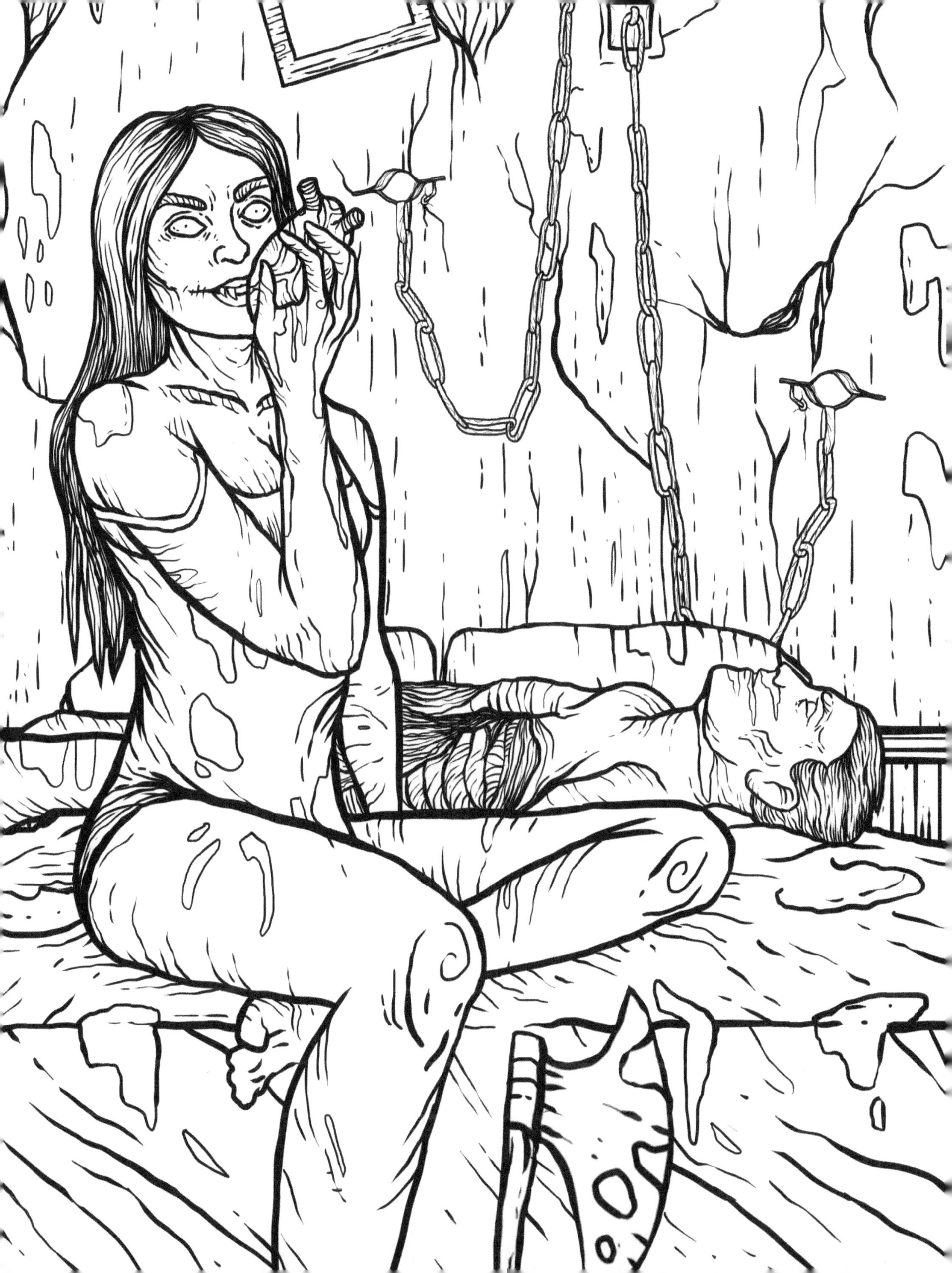

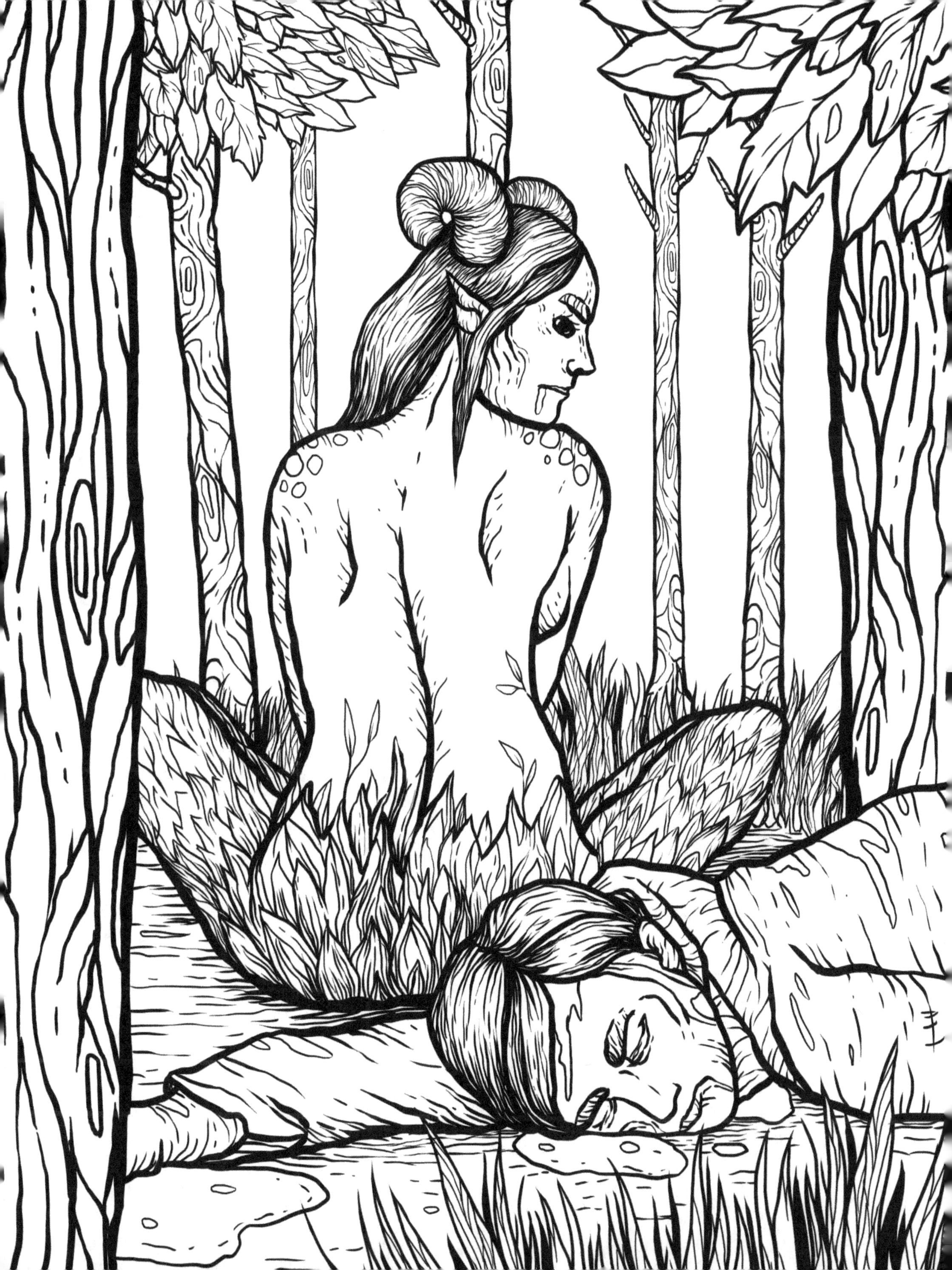

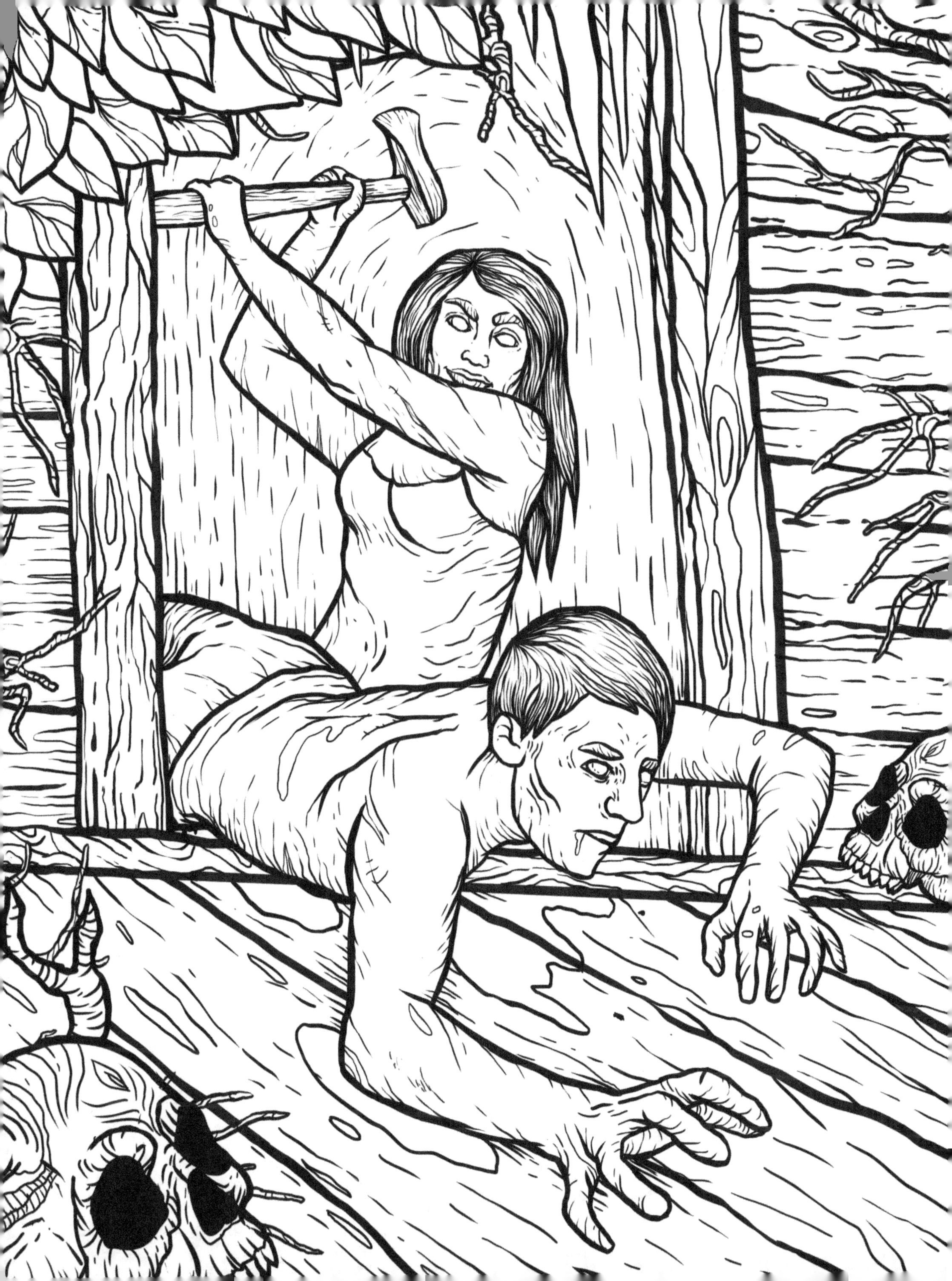

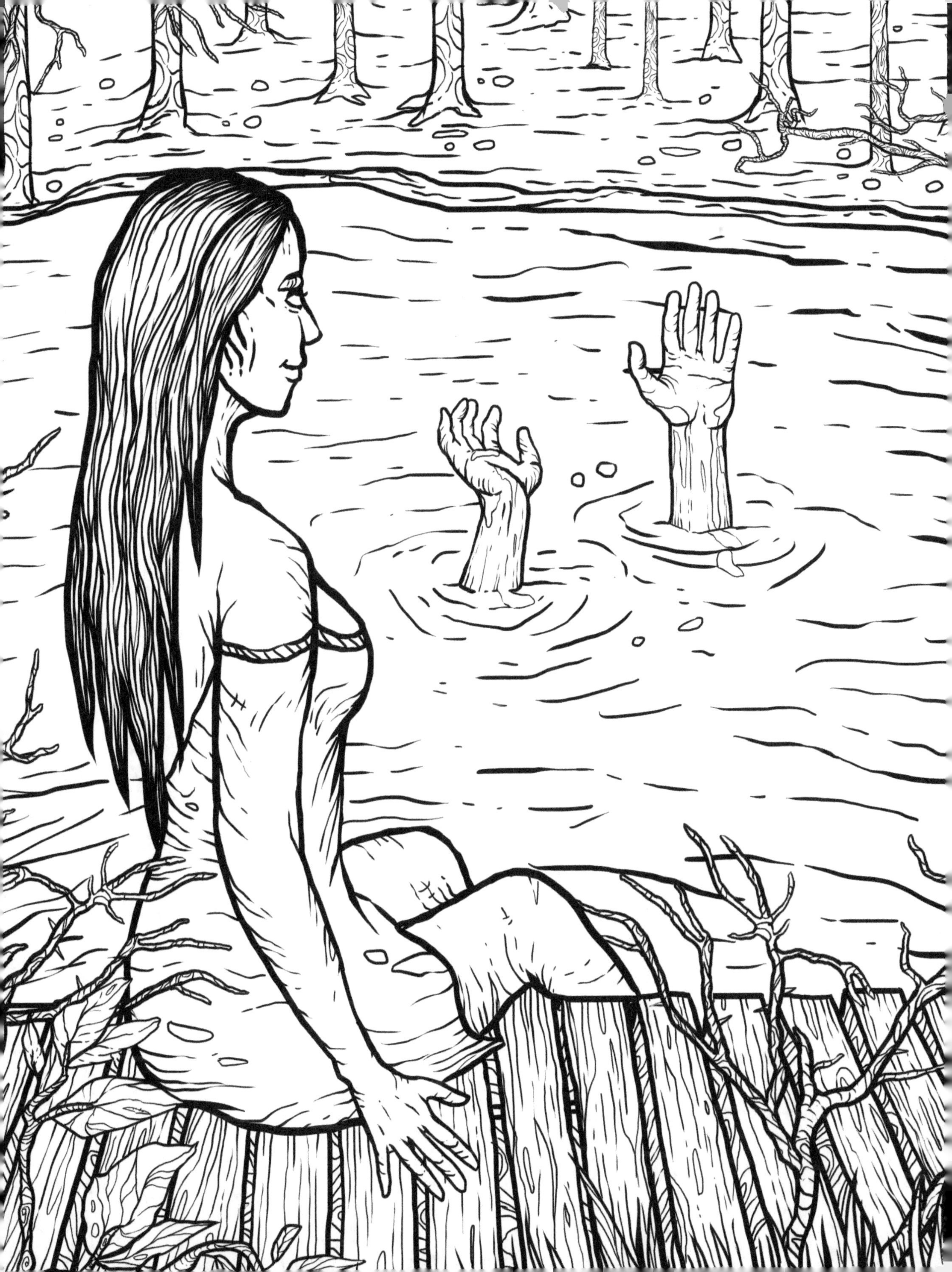

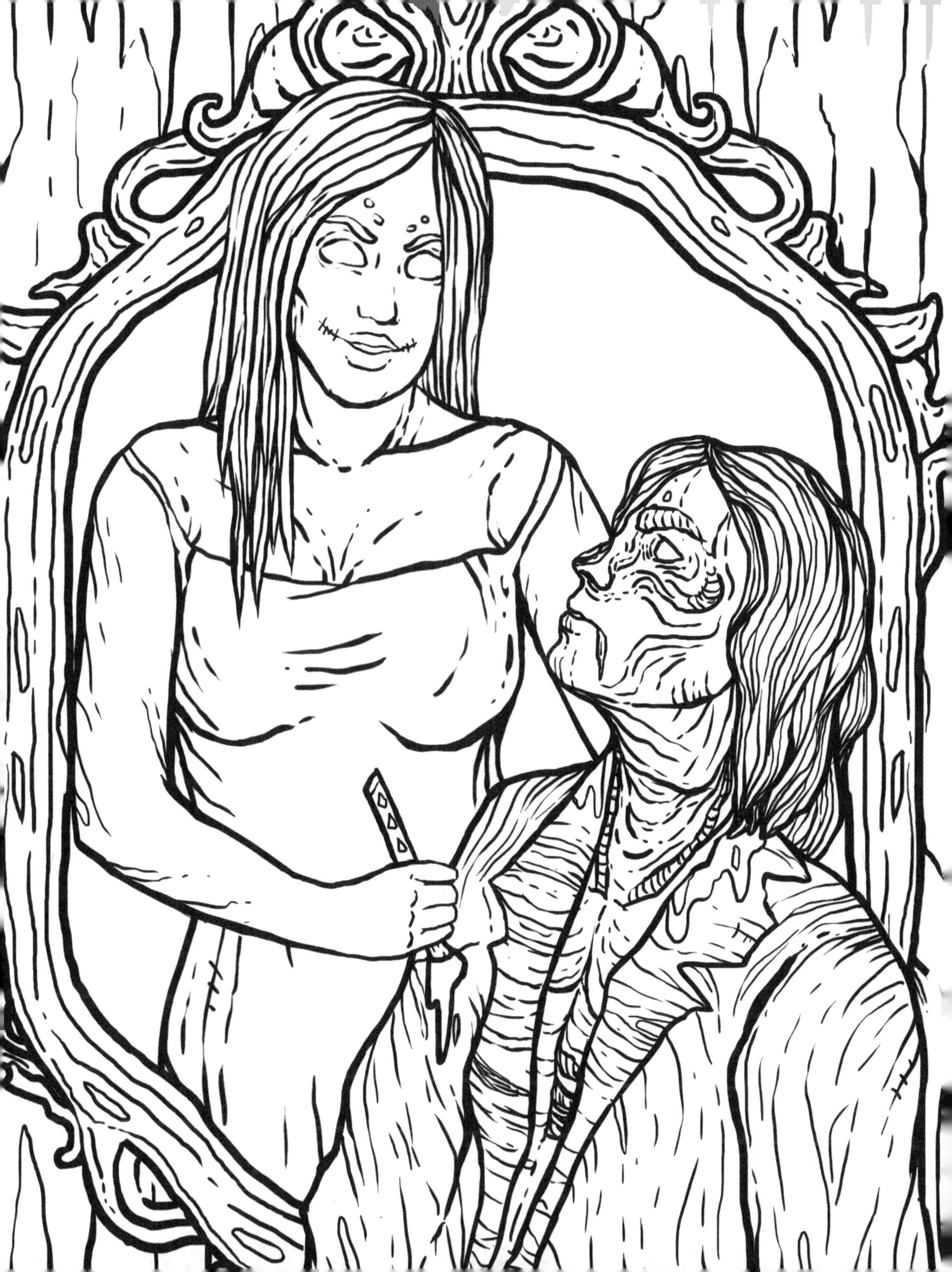

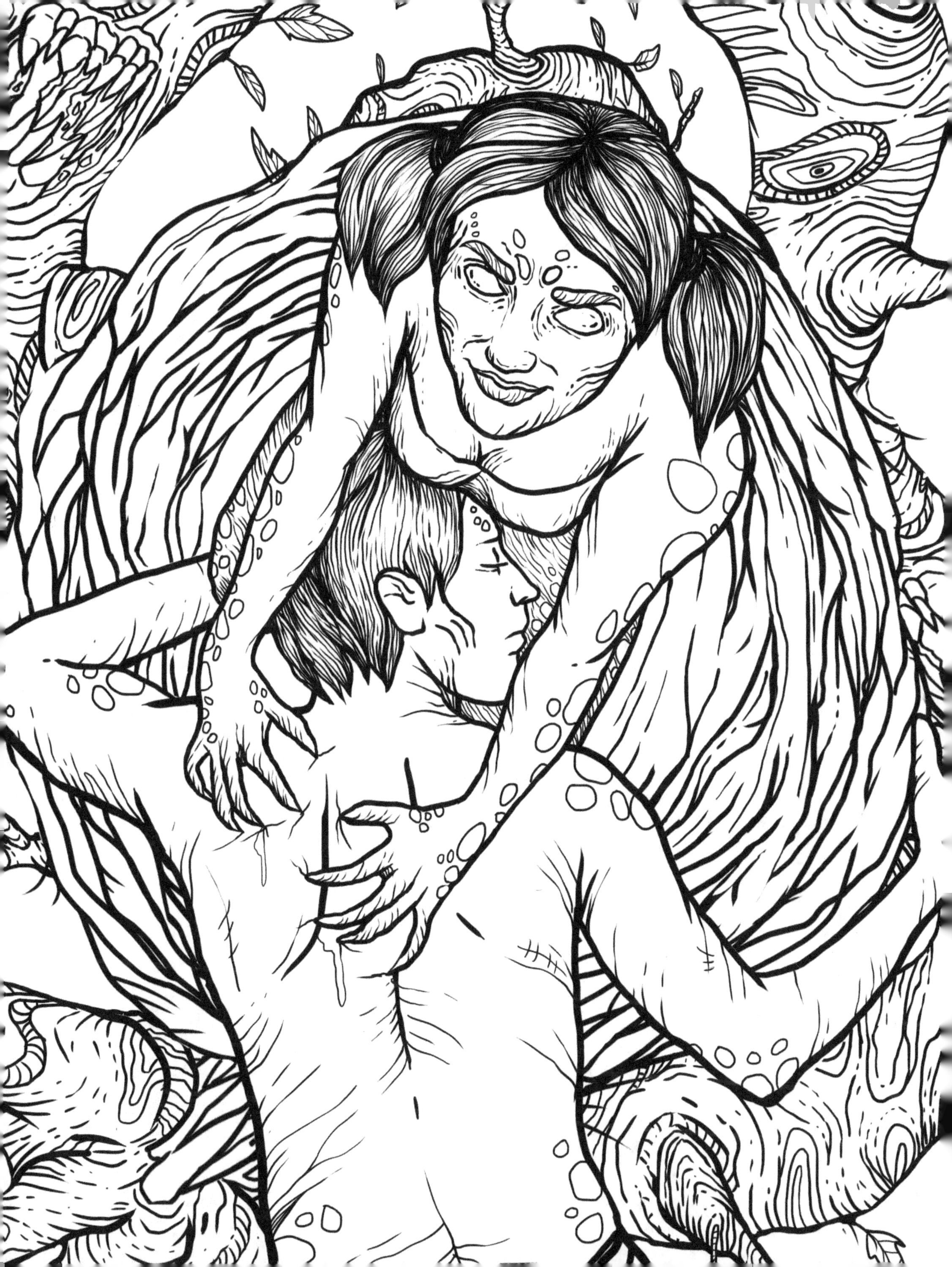

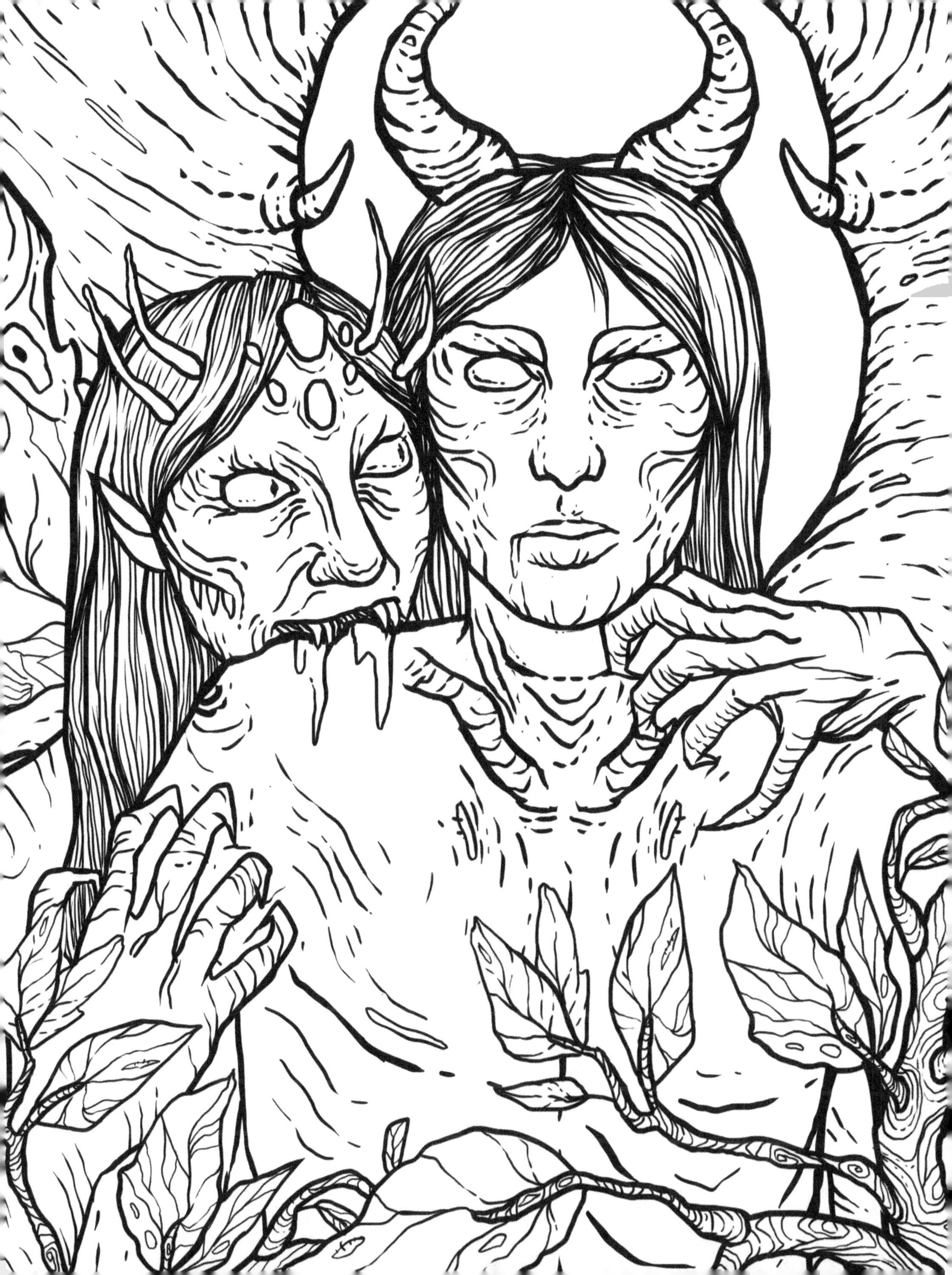

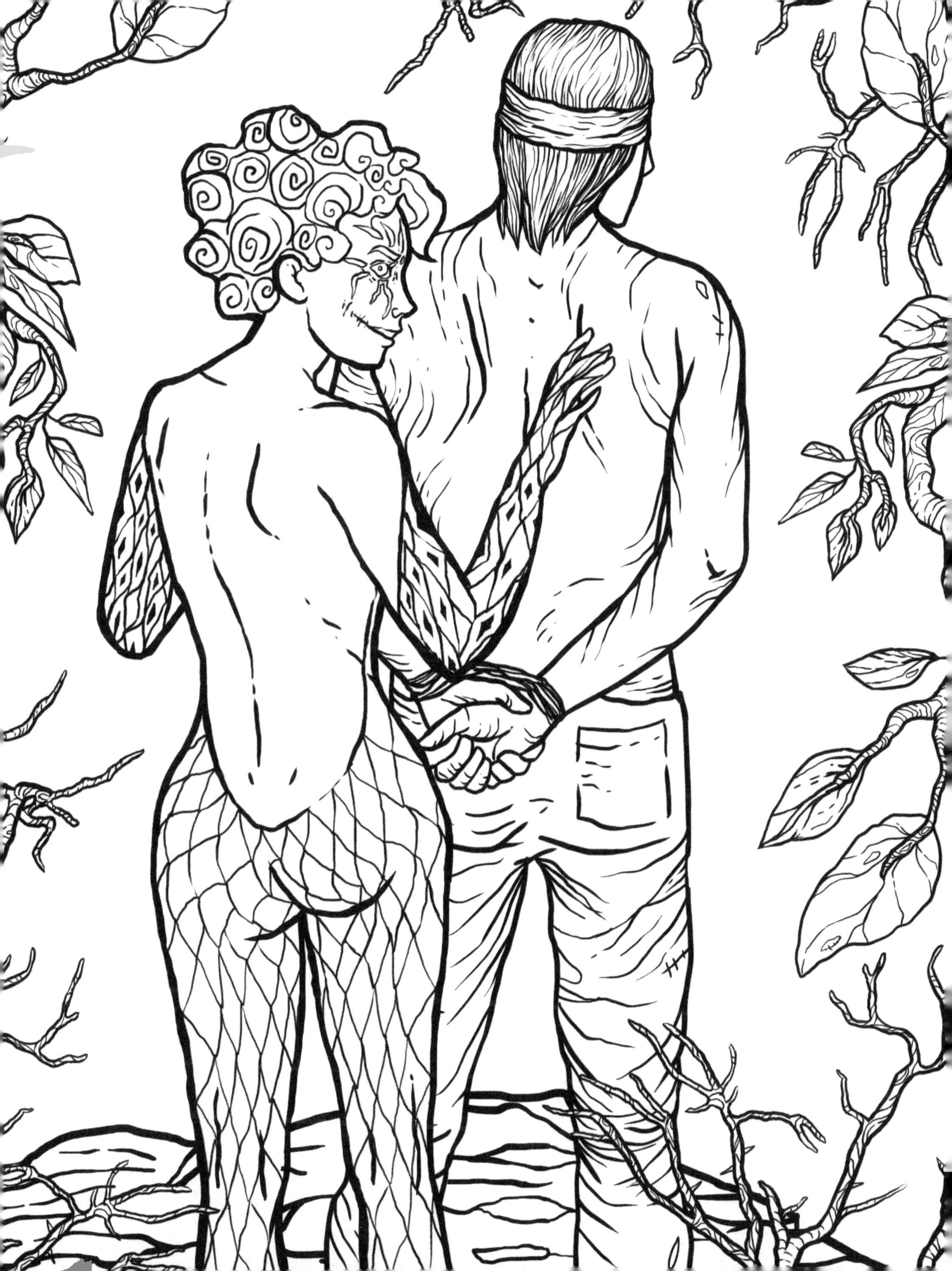

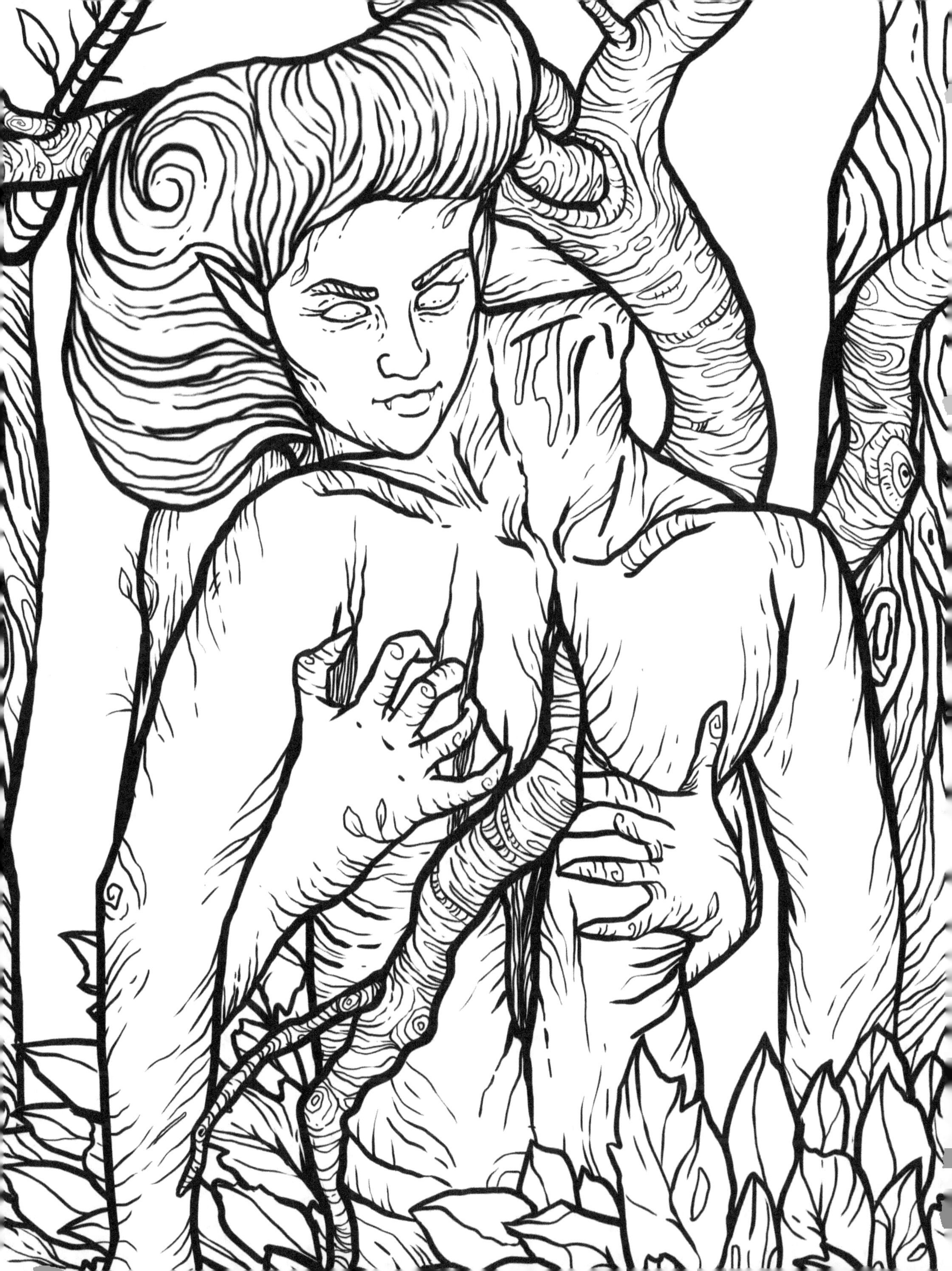

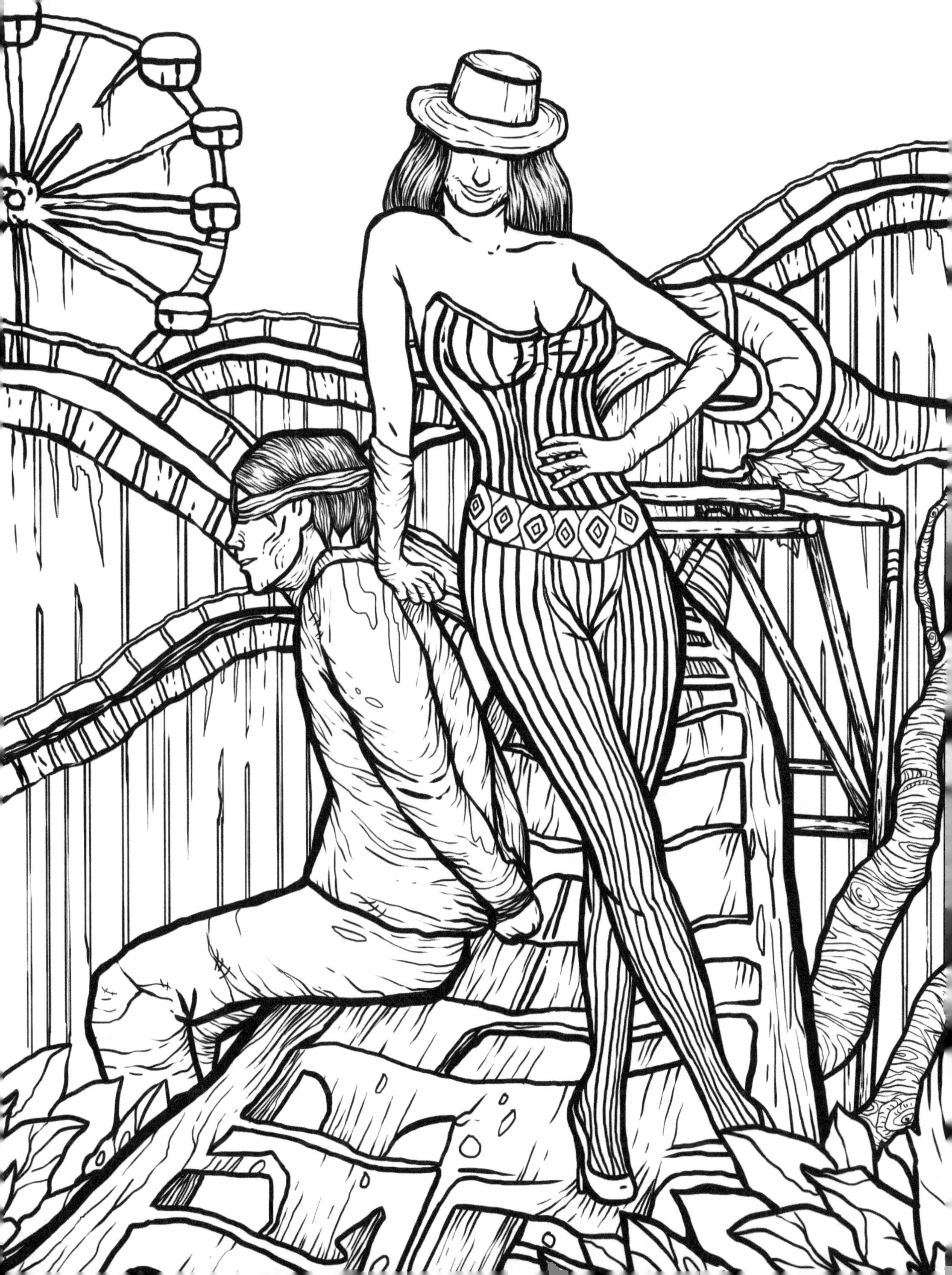

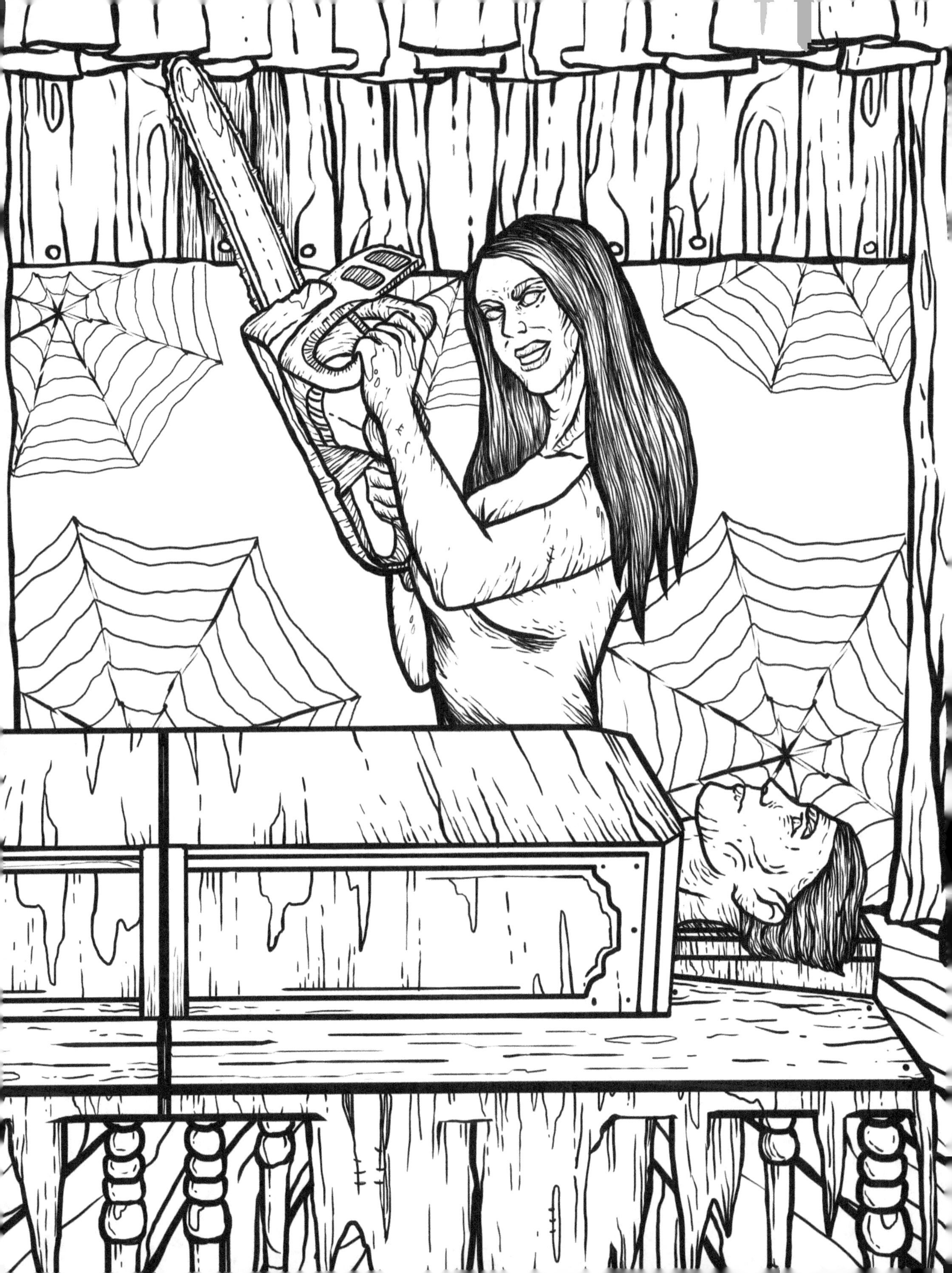

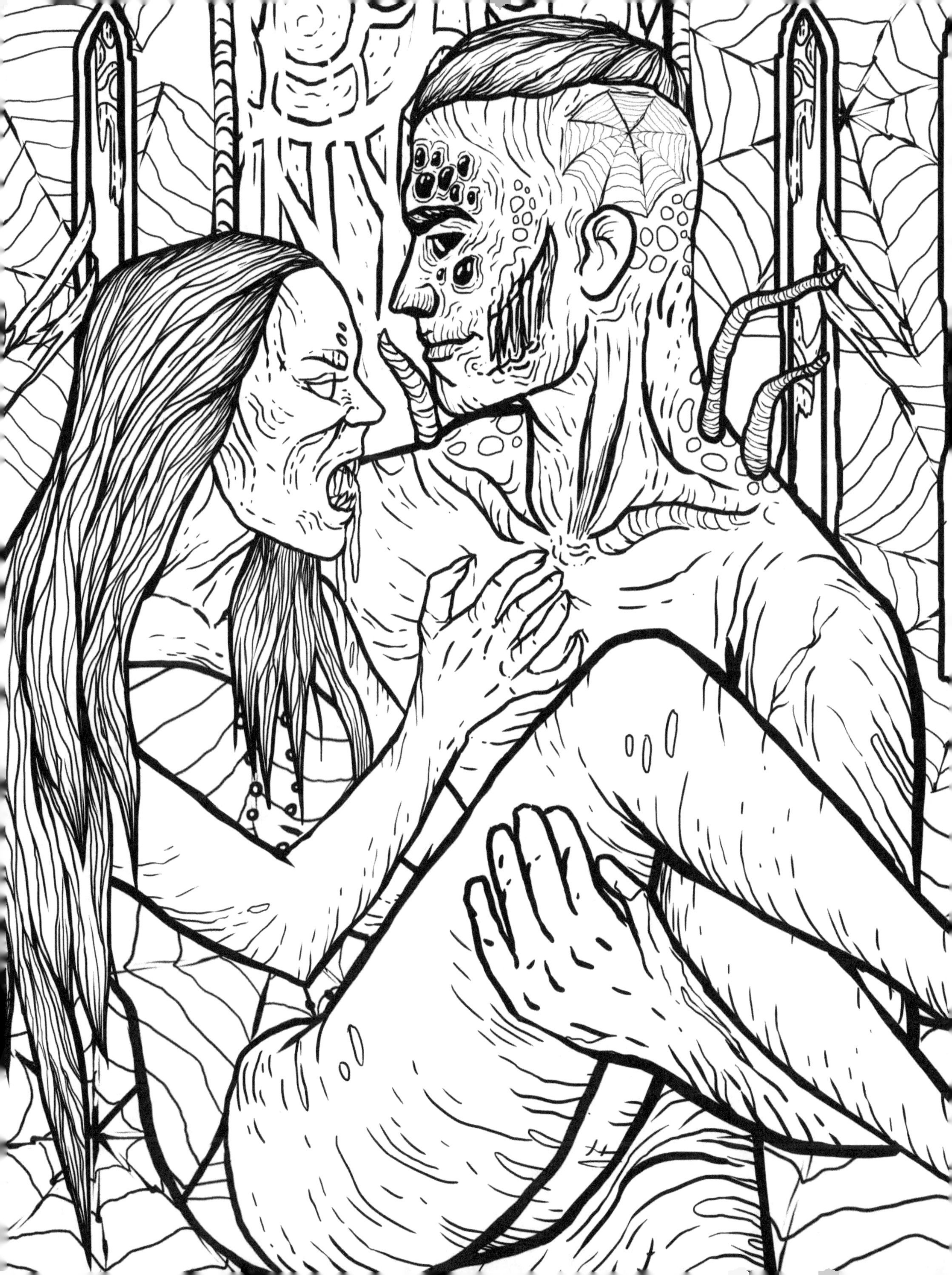

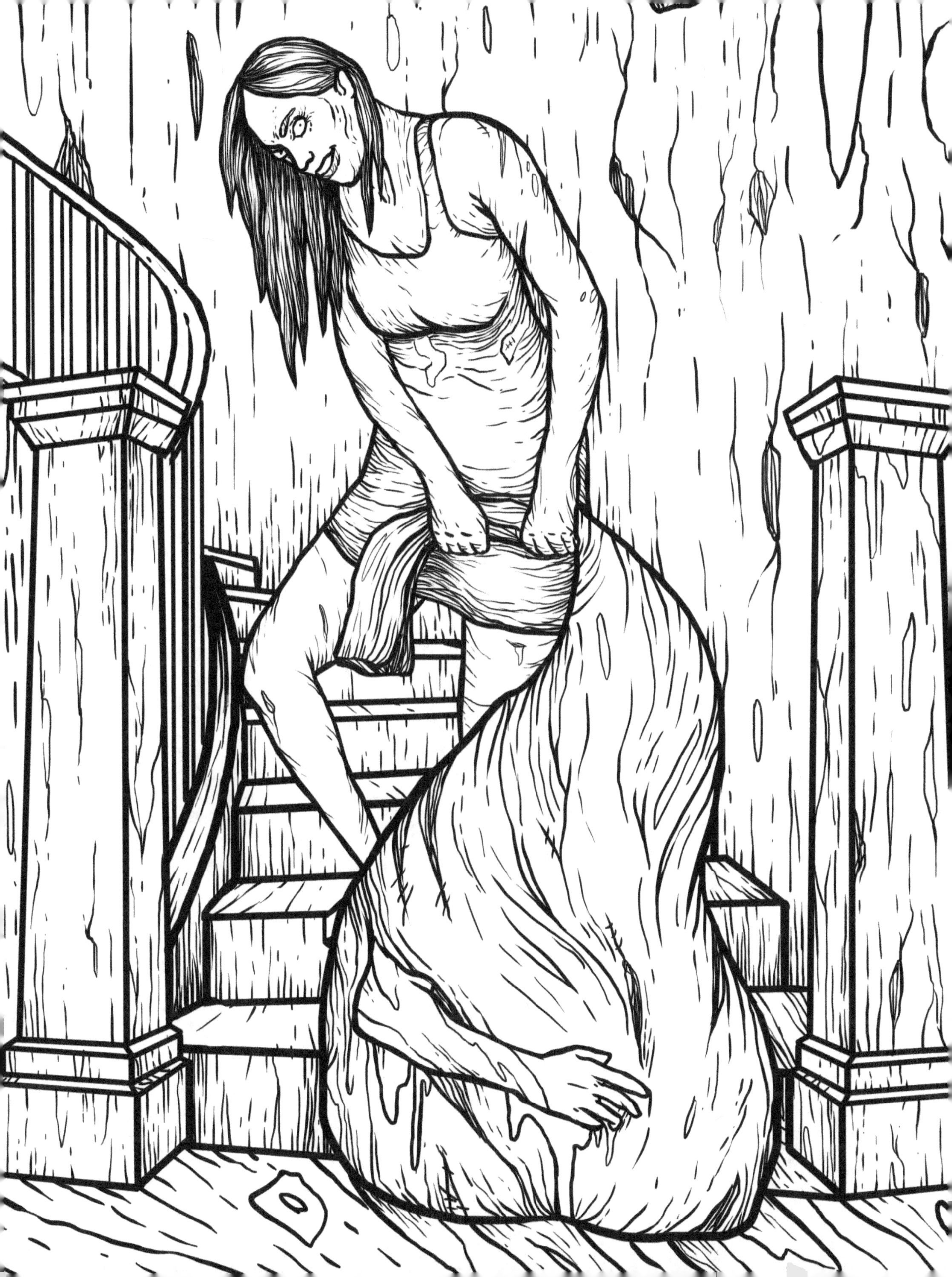

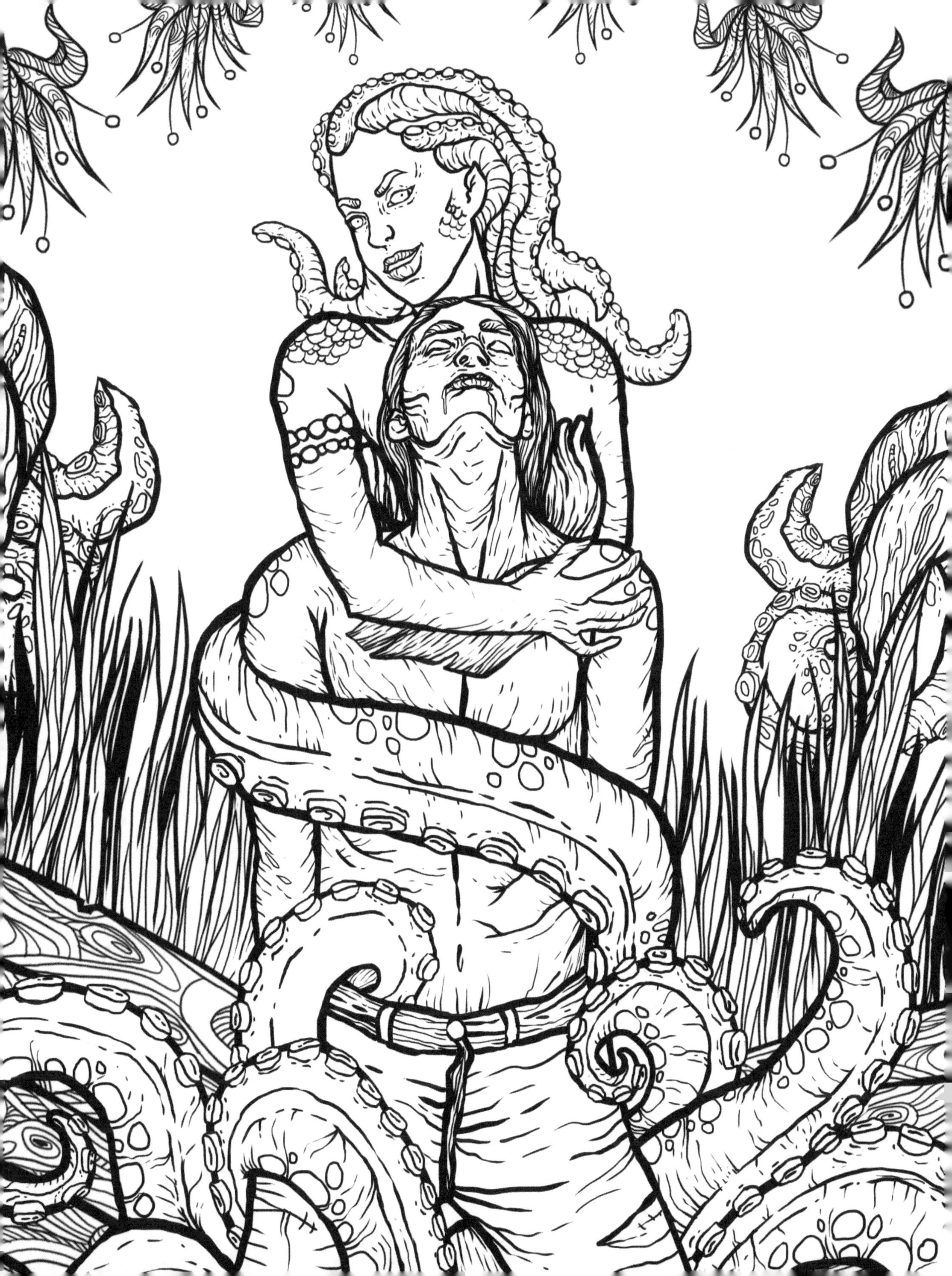

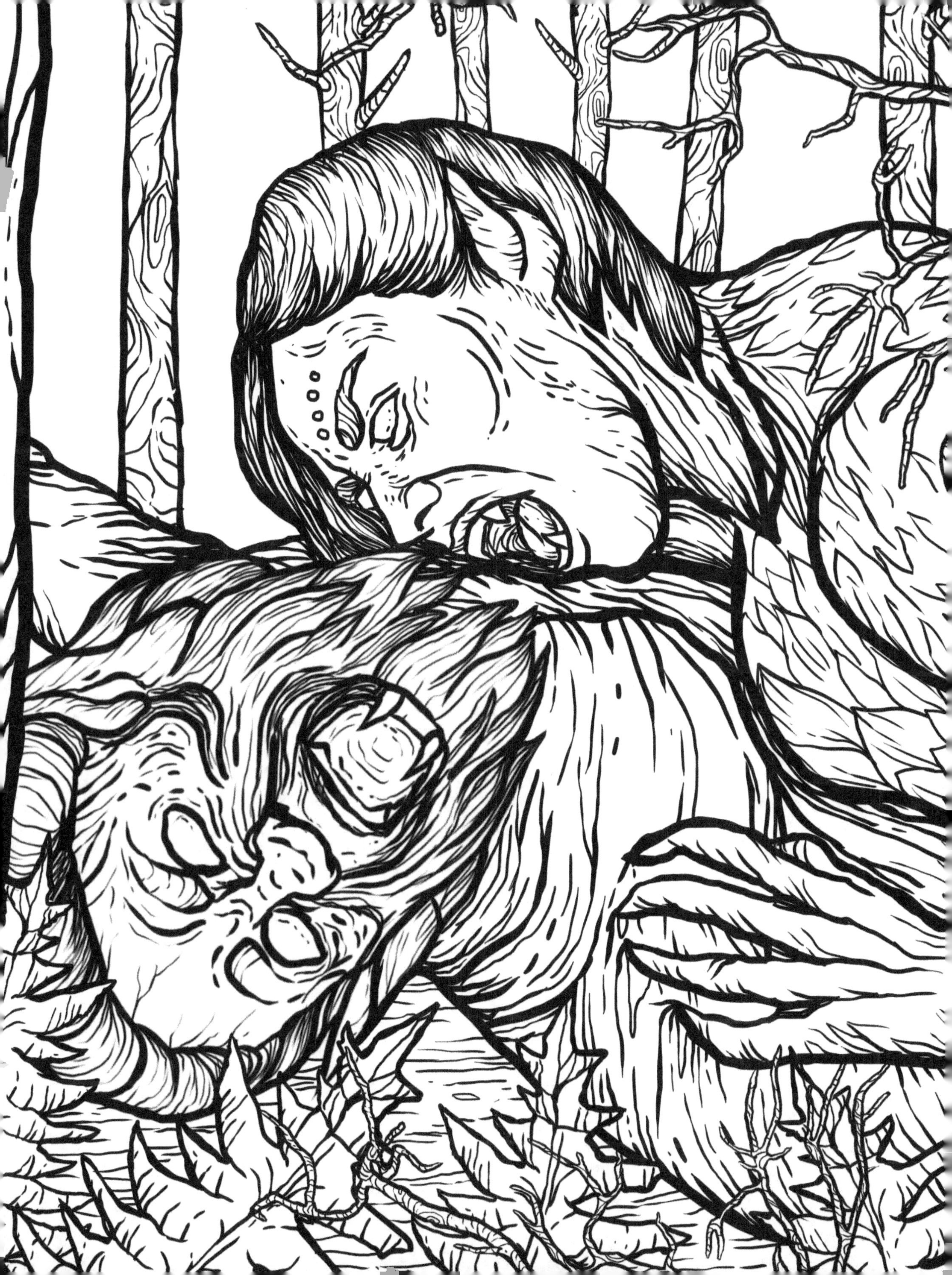

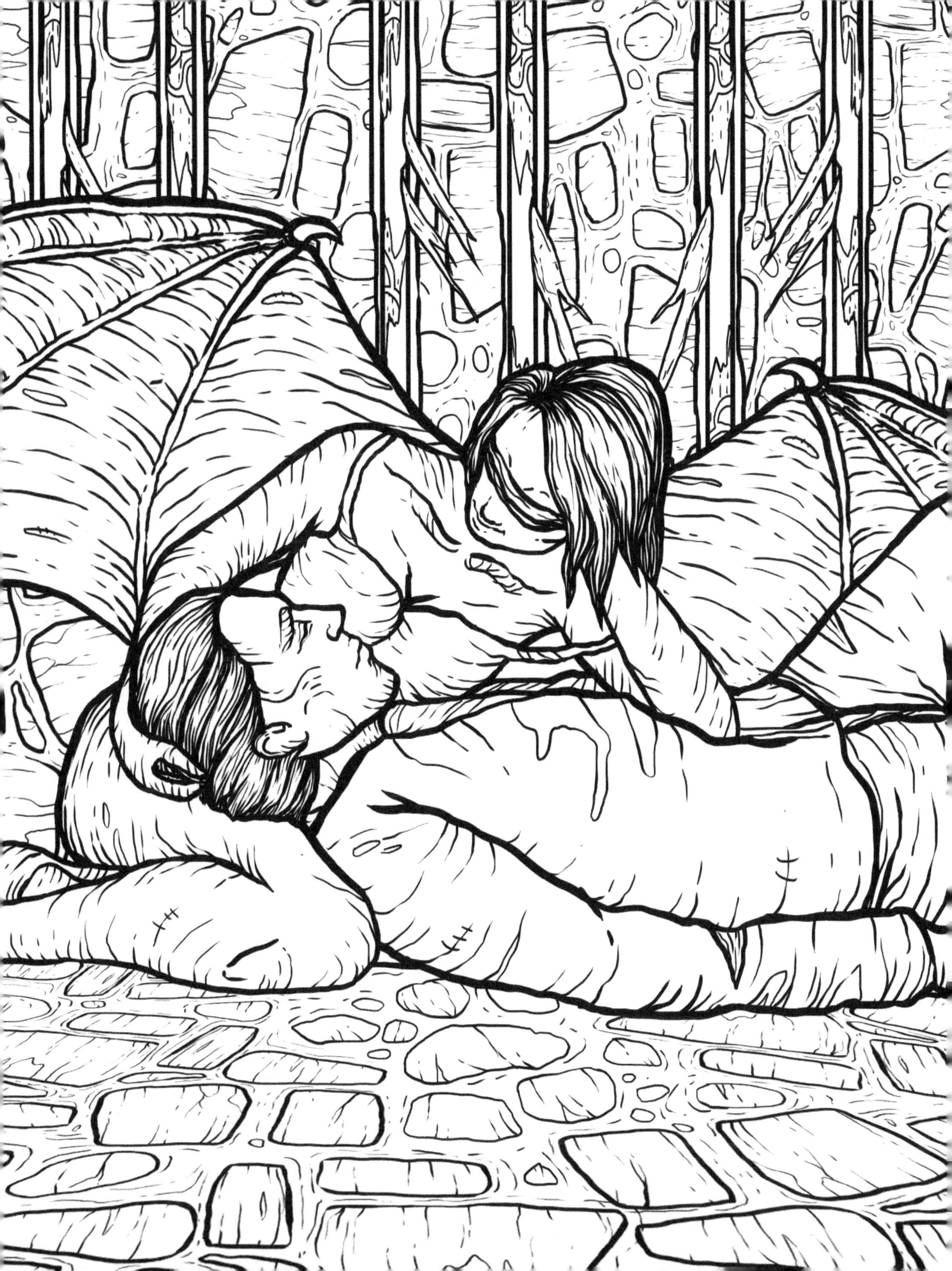

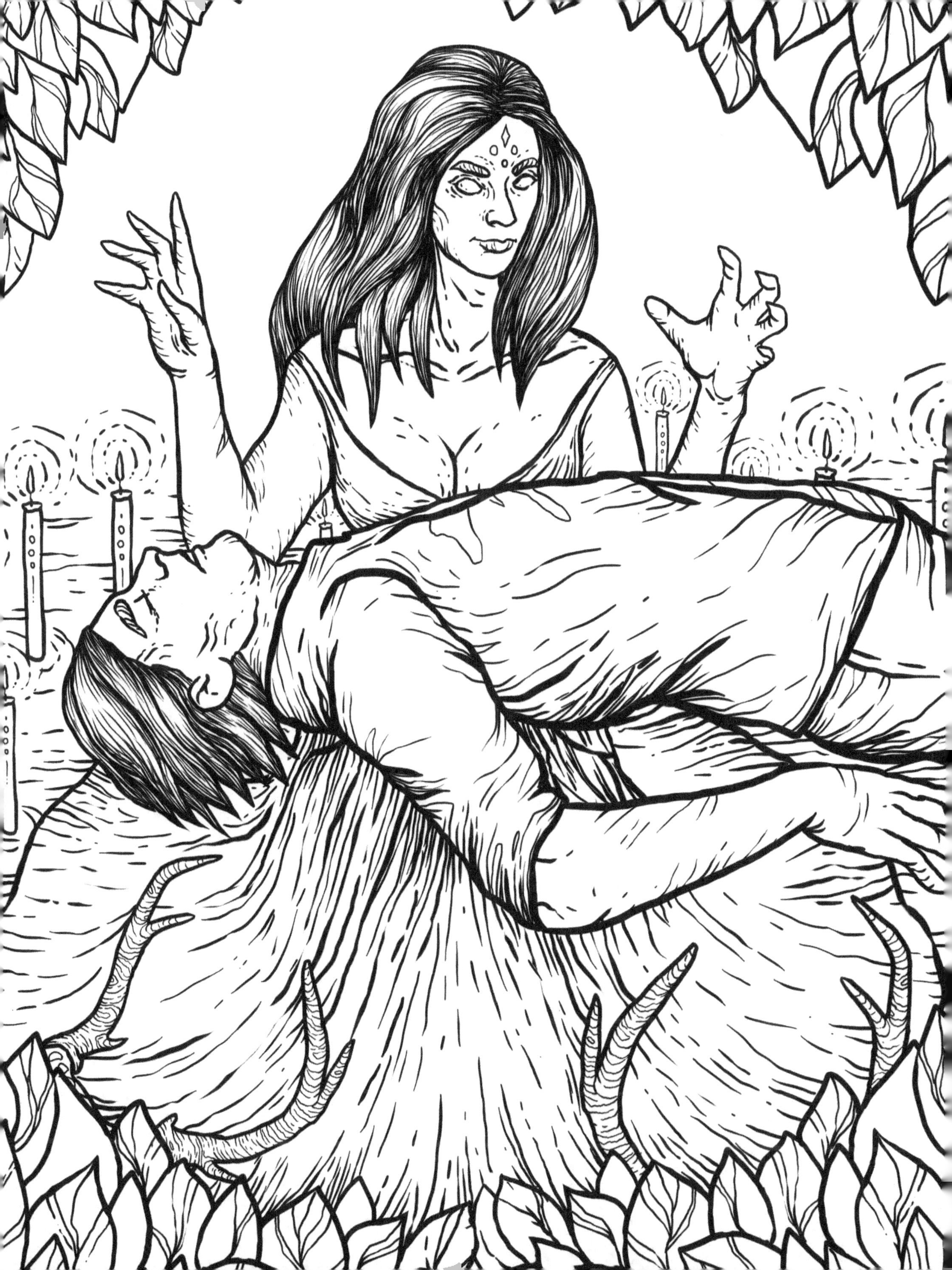

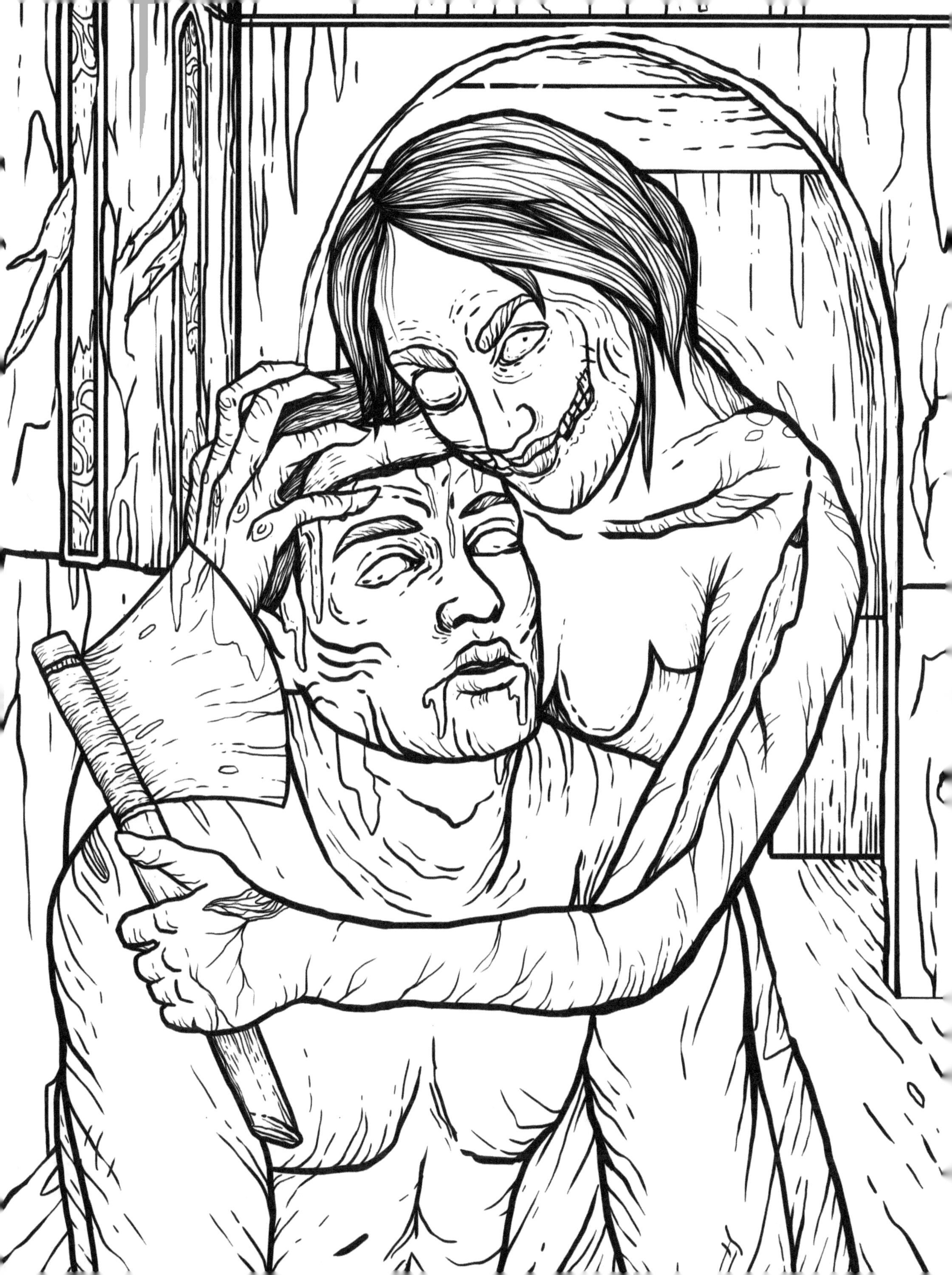